The Little Engine That Could™

Choo Choo Charlie Saves the Carnival

For my brother Mike, who is more fun than any carnival—M.E.B.

To my best buddy boy Zart, with much love—C.O.

Library of Congress Cataloging-in-Publication Data

Bryant, Megan E.
   The little engine that could : Choo Choo Charlie saves the carnival / written by Megan E. Bryant ; based on the original story by Watty Piper ; illustrated by Cristina Ong.
      p. cm.
Summary: After a day of helping set up a carnival, Choo Choo Charlie, who is unhappy about being given only baby jobs to do, offers to fill in for the broken Tiny Tykes Train ride.
   ISBN 0-448-43513-6 (pbk.)
   [1. Railroads—Trains—Fiction. 2. Carnivals—Fiction.] I. Title: Choo Choo Charlie saves the carnival.
II. Piper, Watty, pseud. III. Ong, Cristina, ill. IV. Title.
   PZ7.B83945Li 2004
   [E]—dc22
                                                                                      2003014179

ISBN 0-448-43513-6   A B C D E F G H I J

The Little Engine That Could™

Choo Choo Charlie Saves the Carnival

Written by Megan E. Bryant
Based on the original story by Watty Piper
Illustrated by Cristina Ong

Platt & Munk, Publishers • New York

Mr. John, the stationmaster at the Piney Vale train station, had a big announcement to make. "I've got great news, everybody!" he told The Littl[e] Engine That Could and her friends Engine Eddie, Lucy Locomotive, and Choo Choo Charlie. "The Kidland Carnival is making an unexpected stop, and it's coming to Piney Vale—*today*!"

"Hooray!" cheered the trains. Choo Choo Charlie was so excited that he almost jumped his tracks!

"Now, setting up an entire carnival in just one day is a mighty big job," Mr. John told the trains. "We all need to help the workers however we can." "And we will!" promised the Little Blue Engine.

The trains went to the fairgrounds to help set up the carnival.
"Listen up, everybody," Engine Eddie said importantly. "We should
split up so that we all find ways to help. Lucy, you can help set up the rides.
Little Blue, you check with Stationmaster John about picking up passengers
And I'll help set up the big top tent."

"I want to work with Eddie," Choo Choo Charlie piped up. "Putting up the big top tent will be fun!"

But then Charlie had an even better idea.

"Or *maybe* I can do something that's even more fun!" Charlie said excitedly. "I'm good at making people laugh—I can be a clown at the carnival! Listen to *this*!"

Charlie cleared his throat. "Why is Stationmaster John so busy?" He paused. "Because he has to keep *track* of everything! Ha, ha! Get it?"

Everyone laughed. "That's a great joke, Charlie!" the Little Blue Engine said. "But the carnival already has its own clowns."

Charlie grinned. "I guess you're right. But if the carnival *did* need an extra clown, I bet I'd be great!"

"Well, I've got a job for you, Charlie," said Eddie. "Why don't you move
these boxes behind the station? That's a *big* help."

"No problem," Charlie said. "You can count on me, Eddie!"

When he'd finished, Charlie crossed the fairgrounds to where Eddie and some workers were putting up the big top tent.

"Eddie, I finished moving the boxes," Charlie said breathlessly. "I can help you set up the tent now!"

"Thanks, Charlie, but we've got it under control," Eddie puffed. Then he yelled to the workers, "On my count—one, two, three, *pull*!"

The enormous, brightly colored circus tent sprung up from the ground. It was beautiful, but Charlie felt so blue that he barely noticed. "I could have helped, too," he mumbled. He gave a sad sigh.

Then Charlie spotted Lucy Locomotive and he perked up.
She was helping the mechanics set up the carousel. "I bet Lucy can use
my help!" he said to himself.

He hurried over to Lucy and the mechanics. "Lucy, I'll help you put
together the rides—I can do it!" he said eagerly. But in his excitement, Charli
accidentally knocked over Lucy's toolbox. Tools went flying everywhere!

"Sorry," Charlie said as the mechanics picked up the tools.

"That's okay, Charlie," Lucy said kindly. Just then, Engine Eddie came by. "What's all this?" he asked. Then he turned to Charlie. "Charlie, maybe you'd better leave the assembly to Lucy and the mechanics. Why don't you go get some more nails from the train station?"

"Oh, boy—another *boring* job," Charlie muttered as he chugged away.

When Charlie returned, Mr. John was talking to Engine Eddie and The Little Engine That Could.

"Mr. John, everything's under control," Eddie was saying importantly. "I put up the big top tent. Lucy's setting up the last ride, the Tiny Tykes Train. And the Little Blue Engine here is about to pick up passengers from Maple Falls, Twin Oaks, and Willow Grove.

"And Charlie's really been helping out, too," Eddie continued. "Isn't that right, Charlie?"

Charlie opened his mouth, but before he could speak, Stationmaster John cut in.

"Wonderful!" said Mr. John. "I'm so proud of you all! Now, I've got to check in with Miss Hart, the carnival owner. Let me know if you need anything. Great job, Eddie."

After Mr. John left, Eddie turned to Charlie. "Charlie, why don't you check all the trash bins to see if they need to be emptied?"

"No!" Charlie yelled. "You're not the boss of me!"

Eddie and the Little Blue Engine looked at Charlie, surprised. "What do you mean, Charlie?" the Little Blue Engine asked.

"All day long, Eddie's been bossing me around, giving me dumb baby jobs, and not letting me really help," said Charlie. "It's not fair!"

"*Every* job is important," The Little Engine That Could reminded Charlie. "No matter how big or how small." Engine Eddie nodded in agreement.

But then the Little Blue Engine turned to Eddie. "And it's also important to share big jobs with *everyone*—that way, no one feels left out."

Just then, Mr. John and Miss Hart, the owner of the carnival, rushed up to them.

"Oh, it's just *terrible*!" Miss Hart exclaimed. "The Tiny Tykes Train is the most popular ride we have! All those little children will be disappointed. I don't know *what* we'll do!"

"What happened?" asked the Little Blue Engine.

"The Tiny Tykes Train broke down," Mr. John explained. "And Lucy says we don't have the parts to fix it."

Suddenly, Charlie had a great idea.
"I know!" he said. "*I* can be the ride! I'm just the right size. And I'll go nice and slow so the kids won't get scared."

"Why, that's a wonderful idea!" Miss Hart exclaimed.
"But I don't think your wheels will fit the tracks on
the kiddie ride."

"Well, that's not a problem," Mr. John said. "We'll build a new track. We don't have any spare tracks here, but Charlie can pick some up from the Dogwood Grove station nearby. Can you handle that, Charlie?"

"You bet!" Charlie exclaimed.

"Great," Mr. John said. "I'll just call the stationmaster over there to let him know you're on the way."

Charlie hurried down the tracks to the Dogwood Grove train station.

Mr. Paul, the stationmaster, was waiting for him.

"Here you go, Charlie," Mr. Paul said as he loaded up Charlie's cab with some spare tracks. "Hurry back, now. I hear there are lots of kids eager to try out the new train ride!" He winked at Charlie. Charlie grinned happily and tooted his horn as he pulled away.

Soon Charlie was back in Piney Vale. Everywhere he looked, Charlie saw people having fun at the carnival. Eddie was taking the clowns for a funny ride. The Little Blue Engine was dropping off the last passengers. And the carnival-goers were enjoying the rides Lucy had set up—all the rides except one!

Lucy and the mechanics went right to work setting up the tracks for Charlie. Soon there was a shiny figure eight of tracks.

"That ought to do it," Lucy said as she inspected her work.

"Nice job, Lucy—these tracks look great!" Engine Eddie said. Then he looked at Charlie. "That was a super idea you had, Charlie."

"Thanks," Charlie said.

Eddie cleared his throat. "Charlie, I'm sorry that I was bossing you around today. I guess I liked the idea of being in charge, and I was so excited that I just didn't think about your feelings. Are you mad?"

"No, it's okay," Charlie said. "Little Blue was right—every job is important, even little ones. But just remember: I may be small, but I can still be a *big* help!"

Engine Eddie smiled. "I'll remember. I promise!"

"Ready, Charlie?" asked Stationmaster John. "There's a long line of kids who just can't wait to ride the Choo Choo Charlie Express!"

Charlie grinned. "You bet!"

"All aboard!" Charlie cried. He tooted his horn as he chugged around the special new tracks.

The kids loved every minute of it—and so did Charlie!

When night fell, all the happy, tired kids went home with their parents, and the four trains headed back to the station, ready for a rest after their busy day.

"I did it, Engine Eddie!" Charlie said happily. "I did an important job at the carnival and made lots of kids happy!"

"You sure did, Charlie," Engine Eddie said, smiling. Lucy nodded.

"You did a terrific job," The Little Engine That Could added proudly. "Just like we knew you could!"